Peppa Pig
The Tooth Fairy

SCHOLASTIC INC.

ISBN 978-0-545-46806-0

Published by arrangement with Entertainment One and Ladybird Books, A Penguin Company.

This book is based on the TV series *Peppa Pig*.

Peppa Pig is created by Neville Astley and Mark Baker.

Peppa Pig © Astley Baker Davies Ltd/Entertainment One UK Ltd 2003.

12 11 10 9 8 7 6 5 4 3 2 1   13 14 15 16 17/0

Printed in the U.S.A.   40
This edition first Scholastic printing, October 2013

www.peppapig.com

Once upon a time, there was a clever little pig named Peppa. She was very proud of her teeth.

Grunt! Grunt!

Peppa and her brother, George, knew how to take care of their teeth. They brushed them every morning AND every evening!

Brush! Brush!

Peppa and George loved playing dentist. Peppa would pretend to be the dentist and George would be her assistant.

George's toy dinosaur was the patient.

"What lovely, clean teeth you have, Mr. Dinosaur." Peppa smiled.

"*Grr!*" said George.

One day, after playing their dentist game,
Peppa and George were eating their dinner.
Suddenly, something fell onto Peppa's plate.

Clatter! Clatter!

It made Peppa JUMP!
"What's that?" she asked.
"Ho! Ho! It's a tooth." Daddy Pig laughed.
"But where is it from?" asked Peppa.

"Why don't you look in the mirror?" said Mummy Pig.

Peppa looked. She had a BIG gap in her teeth!

"Oh, no!" Peppa cried. "Do we need to go see Doctor Elephant?"

Ho! Ho! Ho!

"No," said Mummy Pig. "It's just a baby tooth. It's meant to fall out."

"A baby tooth? What's that?" asked Peppa.

"A baby tooth is a tooth that falls out when you're young," explained Mummy Pig. "A new one will grow in its place."

"What should I do with my baby tooth?" asked Peppa.

"If you place it under your pillow, the Tooth Fairy will come. She will take your tooth and leave you a shiny new coin!" said Mummy Pig.

That evening, while Peppa watched television with her family, she kept thinking about the Tooth Fairy.

"When I grow up, I want to be a tooth fairy!" said Peppa.

Daddy Pig chuckled. "What about you, George?" asked Daddy.

George pointed at his dinosaur. "Dine-Saw!" He growled.

Hee!
Hee!
Hee!

"Come on, George," shouted
Peppa. "We don't want to miss
the Tooth Fairy!"
They both ran up the
stairs to get ready for bed.

"What are you doing, Peppa?" asked Daddy Pig.
Peppa was carefully brushing her baby tooth.
"I want it to be nice and clean for the Tooth Fairy," said Peppa.

Snort!
Snort!

Peppa tucked the tooth under her pillow. "Are you sure the Tooth Fairy will be able to find it?" she asked.

"I promise," said Mummy Pig. "Just you wait and see!"

"Good night, Peppa and George!"
"Good night, Mummy! Good night, Daddy!"

Hee! Hee! Hee!

"I'm going to wait up all night for the Tooth Fairy," Peppa said. "George! Let's not go to sleep."

George smiled and nodded.

Peppa waited and waited. . . .

Snore!
Snore!

She could hear something.

Is that the Tooth Fairy? Peppa wondered.

"George," she whispered, "did you hear that? Can you see the Tooth Fairy?"

She climbed down to look at George. He was fast asleep. It was him making the noise!

"I am much better at staying awake than George." Peppa sighed. She settled back in her bed.

After a while, her eyes started to close. She quickly opened them again.

"I am going to stay awake and see the Tooth Fairy," Peppa said to herself firmly.

Snore!
Snore!

But soon she was asleep.

Tinkle! Tinkle!

What was that?

It was the Tooth Fairy!

"Hello, Peppa!" she whispered.
"Would you like a coin in exchange
for your tooth?"

The Tooth Fairy gently took
Peppa's tooth out from under the
pillow and put a shiny coin in its
place.

"What a lovely, clean tooth,"
the fairy said. "Thank you very
much!"

Flutter!
Flutter!
Flutter!

The next morning, Peppa found the shiny coin under her pillow. "Mummy, the Tooth Fairy did come after all!" she shouted, jumping up and down.

"Oh, I wish I had seen the Tooth Fairy." Peppa sighed. "Next time I'm definitely going to stay awake ALL night!"